Text © 2020 The Quarto Group. Illustrations © 2020 Ya-Ling Huang.

First published in the US in 2024 by First Editions for
Frances Lincoln Children's Books, an imprint of The Quarto Group.
100 Cummings Center, Suite 265D, Beverly, MA 01915, USA.
T +1 978-282-9590 F +1 078-283-2742 www.Quarto.com

The right of Ya-Ling Huang to be identified as the illustrator of this
work has been asserted by her in accordance with the Copyright,
Designs and Patents Act, 1988 (United Kingdom).

All rights reserved.
No part of this publication may be reproduced, stored in a retrieval
system, or transmitted, in any form, or by any means, electrical,
mechanical, photocopying, recording or otherwise without the
prior written permission of the publisher or a licence permitting
restricted copying.
A CIP record for this book is available from the Library of Congress.

ISBN 978-0-7112-9533-9
eISBN 978-0-7112-9534-6

The illustrations were created in watercolor, gouache, color pencil,
and collage
Set in Lelo

Designed by Zoë Tucker · Edited by Katie Cotton
Production by Nicolas Ziefman

Manufactured in Guangdong, China CC032024
1 3 5 7 9 8 6 4 2

To Amy, Zoë, and Katie

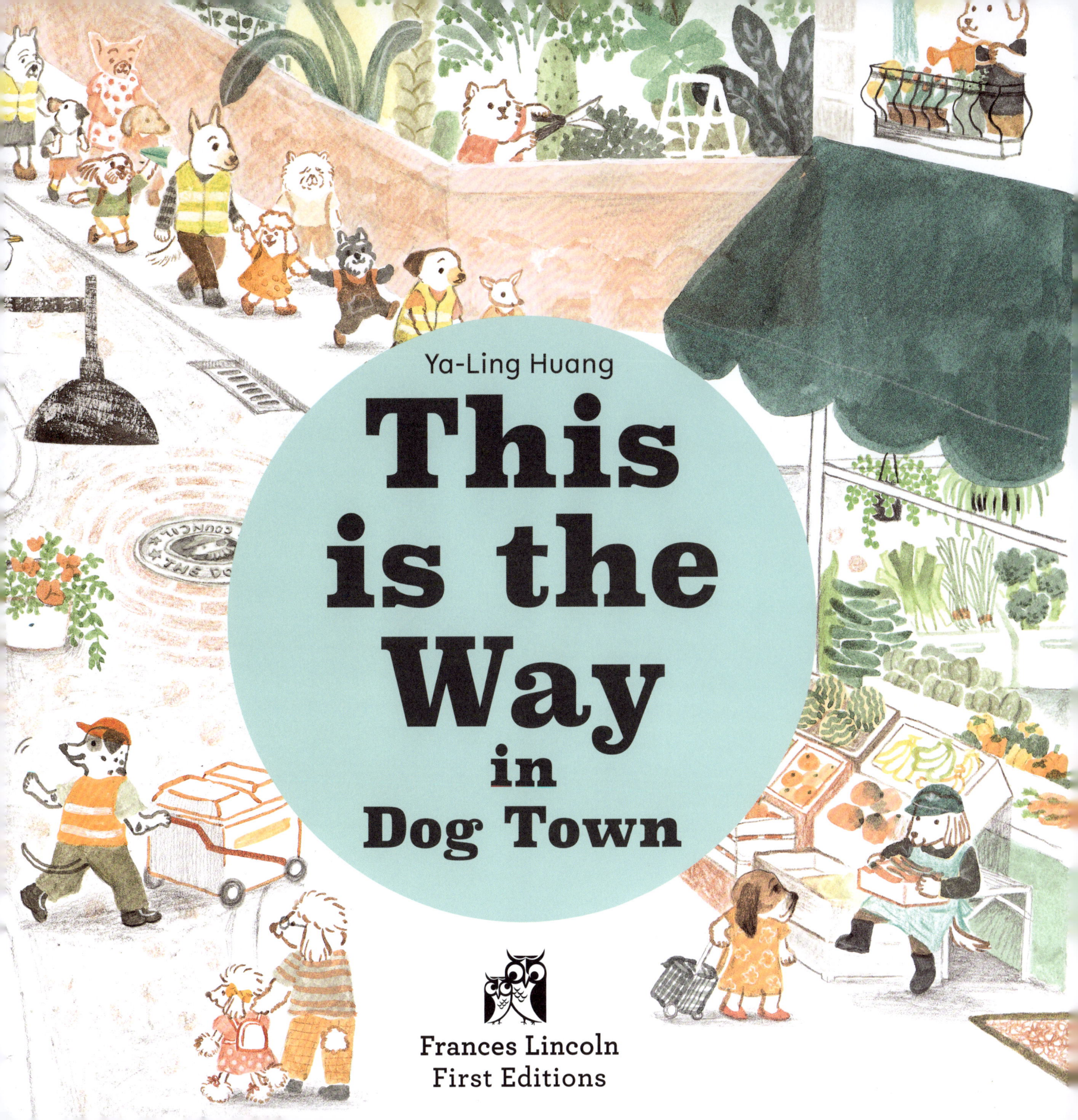

This is the way we brush our teeth,
brush our teeth, brush our teeth.
This is the way we brush our teeth,
early in the morning.

*Brush,
brush,
brush!*

This is the way that we get dressed,

we get dressed,

we get dressed.

This is the way that we get dressed, early in the morning.

Pull,

pull,

pull!

This is the way we go to school, go to school, go to school.

This is the way we go to school, early in the morning.

Hurry,

This is the way we do our work,
do our work, do our work.

This is the way we do our work,
later in the morning.

Draw,  draw,

finished!

This is the way we play a game,
play a game, play a game.

This is the way we play a game,
later in the morning.

This is the way we eat our lunch,
eat our lunch, eat our lunch.

This is the way we eat our lunch,
now that it's midday.

Yum,

This is the way we paint
a picture, paint a picture,
paint a picture.

This is the way we paint
a picture, in the afternoon.

Splat,

This is the way that
we go swimming,
we go swimming,
we go swimming.
This is the way that
we go swimming,
in the afternoon.

Splish,

This is the way
that we go home,
we go home,
we go home.

This is the way
that we go home,
early in the evening.

Walk,

This is the way we eat our dinner,
eat our dinner, eat our dinner.
This is the way we eat our dinner,
early in the evening.

*Slurp,
slurp,
slurp!*

This is the way
we have a bath,

have a bath,

have a bath.

This is the way we have a bath,
later in the evening.
Scrub, scrub, scrub.

This is the way we go to sleep,
go to sleep, go to sleep.
This is the way we go to sleep,
now the day is finished.

Shhhh, shhhh, shhhh.